Sanctuary Lake Home

DAVID E. MALBERG

WestBow Press books may be ordered through booksellers or by contacting:

WestBow Press
A Division of Thomas Nelson
1663 Liberty Drive
Bloomington, IN 47403
www.westbowpress.com
1-(866) 928-1240

Scripture taken from "The Message":"The Bible in Contemporary Language".
Copyright © 1993, 1994,1995,1996, 2000, 2001, 2002. Used by permission of Nav Press Publishing Group.

ISBN: 978-1-4908-0870-3 (sc)
ISBN: 978-1-4908-0871-0 (e)

Library of Congress Control Number: 2013916705

Printed in the United States of America.

WestBow Press rev. date: 9/26/2013

WestBow
PRESS
A DIVISION OF THOMAS NELSON

To my close friends and my loving family, who constantly support me in my literary projects.

David

FOREWORD

I want to thank David and Holly Malberg for having the courage and sensitivity to embrace their Hebrew Roots for such a time as this!

In their quest to grow spiritually, they have embraced **God's Holy Word**, the **Torah** and the **Sabbath!**

It brings me great joy that in all their years of serving **God**, they have finally realized the truth about the **Sabbath!**

They have embraced the revelation that **God's Sabbath** is from Friday sundown to Saturday sundown.

David and Holly have shared with me, many times, how much they learned in **God's Word** since they have joined the **"Relationship Enrichment Center, Beit Tikkun—House of Restoration",** Tampa, Florida.

David's book was birthed while attending our congregation, and it is so well-written that it will bring every reader a great sense of joy!

In **Yeshua Messiah's** Service,

Rabbi, Pastor Hector & Evelyn Gomez.

PREFACE

This is a story of two grandparents (**Taavi** and **Susan**) and two grandchildren (**Tina**, twelve years of age and **Sara**, eight years of age) . The grandchildren are visiting for the summer. This is the **Mohler** family.

The story unfolds during a week in the month of July at the home on the lake in Florida. Pictures of life on the lake will be included.

Scripture and songs will be used to illustrate and enhance the daily activities.

The book of **James** is the primary book of the **Bible ("The Message")** that will be used in this story with selected chapters and verses.

The **Torah** and **Shabbat** (**Sabbath**) are used for teaching purposes.

ACT I

Devotions and Breakfast

Scene 1: Grandparents and grandchildren assemble in the living room the first morning of vacation. This is Wednesday.

Grandpa Taavi: Good morning Tina and Sara. Did you sleep well last night?

Tina: Yes, Grandpa.

Sara: Missy (the Cockapoo) kept jumping in the bed during the night.

Tina: And Gordie (the American longhair cat) kept rubbing against my shoulder.

Grandma Susan: You can keep the door closed tonight when you sleep, if you want. The animals will get used to your being here by tomorrow night.

Grandpa: Tina, Sara and Susan, would you like something to drink before devotions. We have OJ or milk. I have made coffee.

Grandma: I'll fix a cup of coffee.

Tina: May I pour a glass of juice?

Grandma: Yes, you may Tina.

Sara: May I have a glass of milk?

Grandma: You certainly can have a glass of milk.

Scene II: The family settles into the living room for morning devotions. Family goes to the front door and puts the mezuzah on the door post. They read Deut. 6:1-9.

Susan: Taavi, will you please play a few songs for us? Can you include "**Holy are Your Ways O Lord**"?

Taavi: It will be my pleasure to accompany the family with the piano. Tina, Sara and Susan, here are three copies of song books. I will pick some hymns and choruses. (Grandpa plays through several songs, as the family sings together).

GP: Here is a new song that I wrote. Here are words (three copies) for "**Holy Are Your Ways o Lord**" (from **Psalm 77:13**):

HOLY ARE YOUR WAYS O LORD

David E. Malberg

D. Malberg   Psalm 77:13

Piano

Ho - ly are you o Lord! How ex - cel - lent is our God!
God is good to peo - ple who put their trust in His Word!

By your might - y Hand, You re - deem your peo - ple to - day, this hour.
It is good to spend time in your beau - ti - ful House of Wor - ship.

Christ is the One who per - forms mir - a - cles for us all.
I want to be in His Sanc - tu - ar - y at all times.

You make things hap - pen for us now and for - ev - er!
Our God is gen - er - ous in gifts and all Glo - ry.

1. "Holy are you **o Lord**! How excellent is our **God**! By your **mighty Hand**, You redeem your people today, this hour. **Christ is the One** who performs miracles for us all. You make things happen for us now and forever!"

2. "**God** is good to people who put their trust in **His Word**! It is good to spend time in your **Beautiful House of Worship**. I want to be in **His Sanctuary** at all times. **Our God** is generous in gifts and all **Glory**." [©2012 Malberg]

GP: Tina and Sara, here is another of Grandpa's newer songs. (He passes out the words {3 copies} for **"Our Mighty Hope is Jesus"**{**Psalm 61:3**}):

Our Mighty Hope is Jesus

David E. Malberg

D. Malberg

Psalm 61:3

(c) 2012 Malberg

1. "A profound buttress is **the Lord our God**; **His rampart** is impenetrable. Our dear **Friend** is **He**--remain secure within the world impractical. The kingdom of evil intent wants to kill us. His might is sure and abundant; and equipped with **Holy Power**, no foe endures."

2. "We depend on **His strength and power** to reach our goals, always guiding. If He is not on our side, to help us against those not abiding in **His Shelter** and **Tower of His Holiness**, it is failure. Who is this **Man of Galilee**? It is **Jesus Christ our Savior**." [©2012Malberg]

Grandpa Taavi: Today, we will begin studying the book of **James**". Tina, would you like to be the first reader?

Tina: Yes, Grandpa. (She begins reading):

James 1:1 states: "I, James, am a slave of **God** and the **Master Jesus**, writing to the twelve tribes scattered to **Kingdom Come**: Hello! " ("**The Message**")

Grandma Susan: Sara, would you like to read now?

Sara: Yes, Grandma. I will be happy to read now. (She begins reading):

(**Verses 2-4**) "Consider it a sheer gift, friends, when tests and challenges come at you from all sides. You know that under pressure, your faith-life is forced into the open and shows its true colors. So don't try to get out of anything prematurely. Let it do its work so you become mature and well-developed, not deficient in any way." ["**The Message**"]

Grandpa: Let's all discuss these first four verses. Tina, what is the purpose of verse one (1)?

Tina: **James** is introducing the book. He is saying that he is **a servant of Jesus, the Christ**.

Grandpa: You have stated the purpose of the book very well. Sara and Susan, please share your thoughts about verses two (2) through four (4). Sara, can you share something concerning verses two (2) and three (3)?

Sara: Okay. We need to be thankful when we have difficult times. If we are close to the **Lord,** we will be able to handle the trials of life.

Grandma: That is a very good summary, Sara. Verse four (4) tells us to make sure that we plan and take difficult things to the **Lord** in prayer for wisdom. This will help us to make good strong decisions that will bring **Glory to the Lord**.

Taavi: Susan, I thank you for that excellent review. Let's continue to read verses five (5)- eight (8). Susan, will you please read this section?

Susan: Yes, Taavi. (she begins reading): **James 1:5-8**: "If you don't know what you're doing, pray to the Father. He loves to help. You'll get his help, and won't be condescended to when you ask for it. Ask boldly, believingly, without a second thought. People who 'worry their prayers' are like wind-whipped waves. Don't think you're going to get anything from the Master that way, adrift at sea, keeping all your options open." [**"The Message"**]

Grandpa Taavi (GP): Let us pray. "**Heavenly Father**, we thank you for your gift of **Salvation** and your gift of the **Holy Spirit**. We want your help today as we boat, swim and fish. We ask for your safety and protection. In **Jesus** name we pray. **Amen**."

Scene III: GP Taavi fixes breakfast for the family.

GP: Susan, can you and the girls take Missy on a walk, while I fix breakfast. I am fixing pancakes, French toast, and eggs (sunny side up and scrambled). Also, there is cereal and fruit. We have coffee, juice, and milk.

GM: Come on Missy. We're going for a walk. (The three walk the dog up the roadway for ten to fifteen minutes).

(They arrive back).

GP: Did you ladies see the beautiful sunrise? And, Sara, did you and Tina have a good walk with Missy and Grandma?

Susan: Yes, Taavi. We all thought the view was spectacular.

Sara: Yes, Grandpa. Missy wanted to walk all the way to the newspaper box.

GP: So you all are ready for a hearty breakfast. If any of you want cereal and fruit only, I can also make toast.

Tina: Grandpa, I'll have eggs and pancakes.

Sara: Grandpa, I'll have eggs and French toast.

Susan: Taavi, I'll have eggs and pancakes.

GP: Okay, I will have the cereal and fruit and toast.

Tina: May I bless the food? "**Lord Jesus,** we thank you for this sunny day and the food that Grandpa fixed for us. Bless this food to our bodies we pray. In **Jesus Name, Amen".**

(The meal is finished.)

Scene IV: The girls wash the dishes and put them in the dishwasher. Susan scrapes off the left over food into the garbage disposal.

Scene V: The family gets ready to go to the boat for fishing.

GP: Let's all get ready for the boat ride. I'll get the fishing rods. Let's be at the boat in fifteen minutes

GP Taavi: Can you pray, Susan, for our trip today. I brought sandwiches and drinks for the trip.

Susan: "We pray **Heavenly Father** that we might have a safe and enjoyable trip today, in **Jesus Name. Amen.**"

GP: Family, along with fishing, help me to identify the different kinds of waterfowl. I brought my **"Eastern Bird"** book. I will also take pictures.

GM: Girls, let's help Grandpa untie the boat. We'll start in the front and work our way to the back of the boat.

ACT II

Boating, Fishing, and Evening Devotions

Scene I: GP Taavi takes the boat about a half mile down the lake for a possible fishing spot. GM Susan and the girls look for water fowl along the way.

Tina: I see some mallard ducks. May I take a picture?

GM: Yes, Tina, here is how you take a picture. Look in this opening and press this button for the photo. You can check it after you have captured the scene.

Sara: Grandma, I see an eagle's nest. May I also take a picture.

GM: Yes, Sara. Here is how we take a photo. (The picture is taken.) Let's check and see if you captured the scene.

GP: (While stopping the boat at a possible fishing sight.) It looks like you both captured the nest and the scene very well. What I would like to see now is the catching of some bass so we can have supper. Are we ready?

Scene II: GP shows the girls how to put the bait on the hook. And, then, he shows them how to throw out the line into the water.

GP: According to my fish finder, there is a school of fish about twelve feet down. We'll cast our lines here now and see what we can catch.

GM: (After about a half an hour.) Let's go to the cove further up the lake.

GP: Everybody sit down and someone hold Missy. Here we go.

GM: (After the lines are in the water.) Is anyone hungry?

Tina: Yes, Grandma. I will help with the sandwiches.

Sara: And I'll help with the drinks.

GP: Who would like to pray?

GM: I'll pray Taavi. " **Lord**, we thank you for this time that we can spend with the girls. May there be a cloud cover and a breeze to make the outing more pleasant. And bless these sandwiches, we pray in the name of **Yeshua (Jesus). Amein (Amen)."**

GP: Let's eat. Watch your sandwich. Missy will take the whole thing if you are not careful.

Scene III: After lunch, Taavi decides to take the family on a boat ride.

GP: Let's bring in the lines on the fishing rods. This is how you secure the hooks. (He places them carefully inside the boat away from the passengers.) Let's go to the other end of the lake. Would one or both of you girls like to ride on the raft?

Sara: I would Grandpa.

GM: Ok. Let's hook the line to the rail on the boat and connect it to the raft.

GP: Tina, would you like to join your sister on the raft.

Tina: Yes, Grandpa.

GM: Let's make sure the life jacket straps are tight and secure.

(So, one by one, Susan and Taavi help the girls get on the raft. Taavi makes sure the rope is tight and secure and clear of the boat motor.)

GP: Let's go! (Taavi puts the boat in gear and accelerates up to 3500 RPM.)

GM: Taavi, slow down a little!

(Taavi slows the boat to 3000 RPM.)

Scene IV: After going up and down the lake, Taavi decides to take the family into the dock.

GP: Did everyone have a good time?

Sara and Tina: Yes, Grandpa. Can we do this again later this week?

GP: We'll plan our schedule after devotions and after supper.

GM: I'm going to rest a while. Would you girls like to take a nap now?

Tina and Sara: Yes, Grandma.

(Susan and the girls pick up items from the boat.)

GP: Have a good nap. I'm going to fish of the dock for a few minutes. I saw a fish jumping over to the right of the dock. I'll see you in about half an hour.

Susan and girls: I hope you catch something for supper.

GP: Thank you. I'm going to give my best effort.

(As the family walks to the house, Taavi casts to the side of the dock. He tries a couple of places near the lily pads on the right. Then, he casts directly in front of the dock about 15 to 20 feet away. All of a sudden, he feels a tug on his line. He begins to reel it in, and to his amazement, there is a five to six pound bass on the line. After a time of letting out the line and reeling it in, Taavi brings the pole to about two feet above the water and puts his net under the fish.)

Taavi: (He calls Susan on the phone.) Susan, I caught a large bass. Would you and the girls like to see it before you take your nap?

(The family comes back down to the dock. They are happy and amazed at the size and the beauty of the fish.)

Susan: We'll go and take our naps.

Taavi: I'll clean the fish and put it in the freezer and take a nap myself.

Scene V: Susan, Tina and Sara go swimming, while Grandpa fries the bass from the lake on the grill.

Tina: The pool is very nice in this 100 degree heat.

Sara: I love swimming in the pool. And, look at <u>Gordie</u> on the table.

Susan: We're very happy you both like the pool. Grandpa makes sure the pool man Danny cleans and treats the water in the pool every week. Grandpa also makes sure the pool is comfortable for swimming every day.

GP: Thank you Susan. Can you all smell the delicious fish being cooked?

Susan, Tina and Sara: Yes we can. It smells delicious.

GP: I am cooking some fresh vegetables and browning some rolls also. I'll have the food prepared in about a half hour.

Scene VI: GP calls the family to the table. He asks Tina and Sara to set the table. Susan gets the drinks and other items for the meal.

GP: Let's pray: In Hebrew: "**Baruch** atah **Adonai**, **Elohenu Melech** ha olam, hamotzi lechem min ha aretz, lechem chaim **b'Yeshua. Amein**." "**Blessed** are you**, Lord our God, King of the Universe**, who blesses us with bread, **the Bread of Life in Yeshua**."

(After the meal, Susan and the girls wash off the dishes for the dishwasher and put away any food items.)

GP: Let's gather in the family room for our evening devotions.

Scene VII: The family gathers in the family room for devotions, which includes testimonies, music and prayer. Susan passes out the song books.

GP (at the organ): Let's sing some hymns and choruses. (The family sings songs together).

GP: (About fifteen minutes later). I would like that we should sing some more new songs that I wrote. (He passes out three copies for each song):

"Praise Adonai O my Soul" (Psalm 146 & II Samuel 6:12-15)

Intro: " **Hallelujah! Praise Adonai** o my soul! I will praise **Yeshua** forever. **Blessed is Messiah!** Verse 1: I will sing songs to my **God** for all my life! Happy is he who gets help from **the God of Ya'akov.**

PRAISE ADONAI O MY SOUL!

Psalms 146 / II Samuel 6:12-15

D.E.M.

David E. Malberg

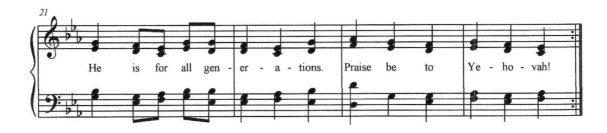

Verse 2: David danced before the **Lord** with trumpet blasts! **Israel** shouted as they brought the **Ark of Adonai!**

Chorus: **Yahweh** is in charge forever! **He is Tziyon's God!** He is for all generations. **Praise be to Yehovah! "** [
©2013 Malberg]

"My Savior Who is My Shepherd" (Psalm 23):

My Savior who is My Shepherd

D.E.M.

Psalm 23

David E. Malberg

Piano

My Sav-i-or who is my Shep-herd al-lows me to be con-tent al - ways!

From qui-et pools, I drink. He guides me to right paths for His Name's sake. A - men.

Praise Him! His guid - ing hand al - ways pro-tects. He is with me.

Din - ner is served. My cup is blest. Mer - cy is set.

"**My Savior** who is my **Shepherd** allows me to be content always! From quiet pools, I drink. **He** guides me to right paths for **His Name's** sake. **Amen**. **Praise Him**! **His guiding hand** always protects. **He** is with me. Dinner is served. My cup is blest. **Mercy** is set. **Life** is with **Yahweh** forev'r." [©2013 Malberg]

(The time of testimonies is presented).

GP: Who would like to give a testimony about our activities today?

Sara: I really enjoyed the lake and the rafting. It was great fun!

Tina: I especially liked the pool. I enjoyed Grandpa's cooking.

Susan: I am thankful for the whole day, from start to finish.

GP: I am thankful, that after six years, that I caught a bass in our lake! Praise be to **Yeshua**!

GP : Before we read the book of James, I would like to read a scripture that relates to the second verse of "**Praise Adonai o my Soul**". (Taavi reads from **II Samuel 6:12-15**):

"It was reported to **King David** that **God** had prospered **Obed-Edom** and his entire household because of the **Chest of God**. So, **David** thought, 'I'll get that blessing for myself,' and went and brought up the **Chest of God** from the house **of Obed-Edom** to the **City of David** celebrating extravagantly all the way, with frequent sacrifices of choice bulls. **David**, ceremonially dressed in priest's linen, danced with great abandon before **God**. The whole country was with him as he accompanied the **Chest of God** with shouts and trumpet blasts." ["**The Message**"]

Taavi: " May the **Lord** be praised for **His Word** that causes us to rejoice and be exceedingly glad."

GP: I need some readers for the book of **James**.

Sara: I'll read first Grandpa. She reads **James 1:12**: "Anyone who meets a testing challenge head on and manages to stick it out is mighty fortunate. For such persons loyally in love with **God**, the reward is life and more life." [**"The Message"**]

GP: Tina, Is there something today that happened to Grandpa that exemplifies this verse?

Tina: Yes, Grandpa, you caught the fish from the lake after six years of trying.

GP: Susan, can you imagine the spiritual, mental and emotional struggles that I had during those six years?

Susan: Yes, Taavi, you struggled a great deal.

GP: "**Praise the Lord** for He answers prayer in due time. **Amen and Amen**." Tina, can you please read **James 3:13-18**?

Tina: Yes, Grandpa. Reading from **James 3:13-16**: "Do you want to be counted wise, to build a reputation for wisdom. Here's what you do: Live well, live wisely, live humbly. It's the way you live, not the way you talk, that counts. Mean-spirited ambition isn't wisdom. Boasting that you are wise isn't wisdom. Twisting the truth to make yourselves to sound wise isn't wisdom. It's the furthest thing from wisdom—it's animal cunning, devilish conniving. Whenever you're trying to look better than others or get the better of others, things fall apart and everyone ends up at the others' throats." ["**The Message**"]

Taavi: Susan, can you please tell us what this passage means?

Susan: We should be healthy, wealthy, and wise. We need to walk the walk. We need to have goals and be humble. We need to be led by the Holy Spirit of the Lord, who will bless us and cause us to prosper.

Taavi: Thank you Susan for that exceptional commentary. And, could you please read **James 3:17-18?**

Susan: Yes, Taavi. I am reading from the book of **James 3:17-18:** " Real wisdom, **God's wisdom**, begins with a holy life and is characterized by getting along with others. It is gentle and reasonable, overflowing with mercy and blessings, not hot one day and cold the next, not two- faced. You can develop a healthy robust community that lives right with **God** and enjoy its results only if you do the hard work of getting along with each other, treating each other with dignity and honor." (**"The Message"**)

GP: Do either of you girls have a comment about this scripture?

Tina: This means that I need to get along with Sara and Grandma and Grandpa and my parents and try to help them and be cooperative. I should operate this way each day. I want to treat each of you kindly and show respect to each one of you.

GP: May you be blessed! Your grandmother and I have been studying Hebrew. Let us pray together a Hebrew prayer: "**Yevarech'cha Adonai** v'yishmerech **Ya'er Adonai** panav eleycha biyechuneka **Yissah Adonai** panav eleychha veyasem lecha shalom". "May **the Lord** bless you and keep you. May the **Lord** cause his face to shine upon you and be gracious unto you. May the **Lord** lift up His countenance upon you and give you peace. (Num.6:24-26) ["**The Message"**]

Scene VIII: The sun is going down over the lake. There are a lot of reds and oranges and other brilliant colors.

Susan: Let's look at the lovely sunset on the lake. (Everyone goes to the dock on the lake).

Tina: Wow, this is fantastic.

Sara: Isn't this a beautiful painting of our Lord.

Scene IX: Susan gets the girls ready for bed. The family has ice cream and cookies. They watch "Ozzie and Harriet", an all American family from the fifties and sixties.

Susan: Taavi, and Sara, and Tina, would you like some ice cream and cookies?

Sara and Tina: (in unision) Yes, Grandma.

Taavi: Thank you Susan. I can help scoop the ice cream.

Susan: Ok. I'll get the bowls.

GP: Girls, after you get your ice cream and get comfortable (while guarding the ice cream and cookies from Missy, the cockapoo , we'll watch a DVD of a family from the 1950's and 1960's. They had a very good home life. However, **Chr**ist and prayer are not mentioned, as far as I remember. But, it is a good, clean show. Today, it is very difficult to find acting performances like we will see on this DVD.

(After the show, Susan asks the girls to brush their teeth and tucks them into bed.)

GP: Good night girls. Please say your prayers before you go to sleep. I love you.

GM: I'll keep the pets away right now. When I check on you later, I'll see if you still want them to be in the room with you or not.

ACT III

Morning Devotions, Canoeing, Swimming and Torah Studies

Scene I: The family gets their beverage of choice and assembles in the family room for devotions. Taavi is at the organ. This is Thursday.

GP: Welcome everyone. I hope you had a nice rest during the night. Sara, can you pass out these music sheets to everyone. I want that we should all sing some more of Grandpa's new songs.

(The first song is presented): "**The Majesty of the Name of Jesus**" (**Luke 2:9-14**):

The Majesty of the Name of Jesus

David E .Malberg

D. Malberg

Luke 2:9-14

1. "**The Majesty of the Name of Jesus** is exalted. He rules and reigns from the highest **Heaven** on earth and in our hearts. How **glorious** is **His name**; it resonates throughout life! **Blessed be our Savior!**"

2. "I love **the name of Jesus** because **He** has completed me. Why should we not serve **Him** and lift up **His name** in every place? How blessed are we who dwell on this earth in our time here! **Holy are you Lord our God**!" [©2012 Malberg]

(The second song is presented): "**Words of Life**" (**John 6:40**):

Words of Life

1. **"Shout the Words of Life** forever, the **beauty of Love** for me. **God's Holiness** for the hearer brings **Faith** to hearts. **Praise Him! His Grace** is so free, secure. **Blessed is the name of Jesus."**
2. **"Send forth the **Gospel of Pardon and Peace** for all men. **Bless Him! Our Lord and Saviour, Guardian** for us ever. **Serve Him!** Accept **His work**, so **Holy.** Let **Him** prepare us for service."

Chorus: "Shout forth praises. Shout forth praises to our **Holy Lord. Accept His Call.**" [©2012 Malberg]

GP: Susan, would you please start reading **James 4:7-8**?

Susan: Yes, Taavi. (reading): "So let **God** work his will in you. Yell a loud <u>no</u> to the Devil and watch him scamper. Say a quiet <u>yes</u> to **God** and he'll be there in no time. Quit dabbling in sin. Purify your inner life. Quit playing the field." **("The Message")**

GP: Sara, what does this portion of scripture mean to you?

Sara: It means that we have to take a stand against sin. We need to be pure and not be divided in our allegiance. If we are to serve **God**, then we need to do so with all our heart. Let **God** do **His will** in us.

Susan: You have summarized those verses well. Tina, would you like to read the next portion of scripture?

Tina: Yes, Grandma. She reads **James 4:9-10:**

"Hit bottom, and cry your eyes out. The fun and games are over. Get serious, really serious. Get down on your knees before the **Master.** It's the only way you'll get on your feet." **("The Message")**

GP: So, when we have reached the end of our capabilities, we need to fall on our knees before **Yeshua, our Messiah,** and confess our sins and weaknesses, and allow **Him** to help us get on our feet.

GP: Susan, will you lead us in prayer for the day of canoeing and swimming, and also bless the food.

Susan: "Thank you **Adonai, our Saviour,** for **your Word.** Help us to stay free from sin and a divided mind. Help us to keep your **Holy Spirit** in the forefront of our lives so that we can be pure and holy before you. Bless our activities this day and this food, which we are about to partake. In the precious name of **Yeshua. Amen.**

Scene II: The family has breakfast of eggs, toast, pancakes, cereal, and fruit. The dishes are cleared.

Scene III: Everyone gets ready to go on the canoe for an hour on the lake.

GP: Let's get on our swimming suits and meet at the canoe in fifteen minutes.

(On the way to the boat, Tina spots something in the cypress tree.)

Tina: There's a bird high up in the tree.

GP: I believe that it is a short-tailed hawk.

Susan: It's probably looking for something to eat.

Sara: Is that why the hawk is so high up in the tree to spot some animal for lunch?

GP: Yes, Sara. The hawk has very keen eyes and can see smaller animals from great heights.

GP: Susan, let's help the girls and Missy into the canoe. After they are in and secure with their life jackets fastened, then, I will help you get in.

Susan: Ok, Taavi. Girls, let's get you comfortable and make sure your life jackets are on snuggly. I'm ready to get in now, Taavi.

Taavi: Ok, let me help you, Susan. Be careful with the rocks. I'll push off and climb in myself as soon as you are safely seated. Here's Missy. (Taavi hands the dog to Susan.)

(The canoe is pushed off and Taavi climbs in.)

Sara: Look everyone. There's a hot-air balloon over the lake.

Tina: May I take a picture.

GP: Yes, Sara. Here's the camera. Grandma will help you set it.

Tina: Ok, I am taking the picture. Grandma, can you check and see if I got a good image.

Susan: Yes, Tina. It came out well.

(The family rows around the lake for about an hour and comes back to shore.)

GP: Did everyone enjoy the quiet ride over the lake?

Tina and Sara : (in unison) Yes, we did Grandpa!

Susan: Thank you, Taavi. It was a very nice canoe ride.

Scene IV: Everyone goes into the pool for a refreshing swim.

GP: After we finish swimming, I'll fix lunch.

Scene V: Taavi fixes turkey burgers, baked beans, potato salad and bread. Susan gets the drinks.

Taavi: Tina, can you please pray for the meal.

Tina: "Thank you **Heavenly Father** for this delicious meal that Grandpa has made from **Your** provision, in **Jesus Name. Amen**."

Scene VI: Family takes a nap and prepares for the evening at synagogue of the Torah Studies.

Scene VII: Family gets ready and gets in the vehicle for trip to the sanctuary. At the congregation, Taavi puts on his **tallit** and **kipa**.

Sara: What exactly are Torah Studies?

GP: They are scriptures from the first five books of the Bible, called the Pentateuch. These books are guidelines and instructions for us as **Messianic Christians** to live a **Holy** and peaceful life.

Scene VIII: At the Beit Tikkun congregation. This is a church that Rachel, the Mohler's daughter also attends. Rabbi Ya'akov and Pastor Debra are presiding. Rabbi tells us that this week's **Parsha (Torah Portion)** is called **Shoftim (Judges).**

(There is a time of worship. Also, the collection of tithes and offerings take place.)

Rabbi: "This portion talks about the connection between justice and righteousness":

"Appoint judges [**shoftim**] and officers, organized by tribes, in all the towns that **God**, your **God**, is giving you. They are to judge [**shafat**] the people fairly and honestly [**tzedek mishpat**/ righteous judgment]." (**Deuteronomy 16:18**) (**"The Message"**)

The theme of justice [**tzedek**] is repeated twice in verse 20:

"The right! The right! Pursue only what's right [**tzedek tzedek tirdof**/justice justice pursue]! It's the only way you can really live and possess the land that **God** [**YHVH**}, your **God**, is giving you." (**Deut. 16:20**) ("**The Message**")

Rabbi points out: in Hebrew, justice (**tzedek**) is related to the idea of righteousness and holiness.

To emphasize, "the words righteous (**tzadik**) and charity (**tzedakah**) are related to justice (**tzedek**)."

Consequently," **God**, who is holy and righteous, is also just."

"He is called the Lord our Righteousness (**YHVH Tzidkenu**), the Righteous God (**Elohim Tzadik),** and Righteous Judge (**Shofant Tzadik**)."

Rabbi asked the question: "What is the end result of justice and righteousness?"

"Peace (**shalom**) and security!"

"And where there's Right [**tzedakah**/righteousness], there'll be Peace and the progeny of Right: quiet lives and endless trust." (Isaiah 32:17) (**"The Message"**)

Rabbi Ya'akov concludes this section: "We can see why it's so important that everyone in a position of authority needs to be righteous and just, including our government leaders and officials, bosses, teachers and, even, fathers and mothers.

(The Rabbi continues this theme throughout the sermon and concludes with this and other scriptures):

"Don't be nitpickers; use your head—and heart!—to discern what is right, to test what is authentically right." (**John 7:24**) ("**The Message**")

Scene IX: Rabbi Ya'akov and Pastor Debra greet Sara and Tina and the Mohlers (Taavi and Susan). The family, then, drives to "Steak 'N Shake" for hamburgers and shakes. Then, they drive home.

Sara and Tina: Thanks for the delicious supper.

GP: Your very welcome. You deserve this treat because you sat through your first Torah Study patiently and you listened well.

Susan: What did you girls think about the **Torah** study (sermon)?

Sara: It was very complicated.

Tina: You have to follow your **Bible** closely to understand what Rabbi is saying.

GP: And that's exactly why **Rabbi** has "**Torah** Studies" to help us understand better **Yahweh's** instructions to us.

Scene X: The girls and Taavi and Susan get ready for bed.

Susan and Taavi: Good night Sara and Tina. Sleep well. Please say your prayers before you go to sleep. We love you very much.

ACT IV

Morning Devotions, Fishing, Swimming, and Sabbath (Shabbat) Supper

Scene I: The coffee is prepared, juice and milk are poured. The family gathers in the Living Room for morning devotions. This is Friday.

GP: Good morning ladies. I trust that you had a good night's sleep.

Tina and Sara: Yes, Grandpa. We slept well. We were very tired.

Susan: It takes energy to study **God's Word**!

GP: Because tonight is the beginning of **Sabbath**, let's sing some **Jewish** songs together.

Scene II: Grandpa Taavi picks out some Messianic Jewish songs in Hebrew and English for the family to sing. He is at the piano. Then, the scripture reading begins, ending with prayer.

GP: Let's continue with the book of **James 4:11-12**. Let's read together:

"Don't bad-mouth each other, friends. **It's God's Word, His Message, his Royal Rule**, that takes a beating in that kind of talk. You're supposed to be honoring the **Message,** not writing graffiti all over it. **God** is in charge of deciding human destiny. Who do you think you are to meddle in the destiny of others?" **("The Message")**

Susan: Taavi, I would like to interpret these verses, if it is alright.

Taavi: Absolutely. Girls, please listen carefully to Grandma.

GM: We need to say nice things about other people. According to the **Word of the Lord**, we need to honor **His Message**. We do this by thinking of others better than ourselves.

Tina: That is not so easy, Grandma.

Sara: No, it is not Tina. That's why praying and staying in the **Word i**s so important.

GP: I would like to pray for us and our day: "Lord Jesus, You have blessed us with good weather, fun activities, good food, and enjoyable family time each day, so far this week. Help us to enjoy fishing, and catching some fish, if it be **Your Will**. Give us peace and safety with the lines and hooks as we are on the dock. Bless our food now that we are about to eat. Also, please prepare our hearts for **Shabbat** supper. We pray all these things in **Yeshua's blessed Name. Amen**."

Scene III: Family eats the food: turkey sausage, turkey bacon, eggs, fruit, toast, and cereal.

Scene IV: Taavi gets the fishing poles out and heads to the dock.

Taavi: Susan, as soon as the girls are ready, please come and join me on the dock.

Susan: Ok, Taavi, we'll be right there.

GP: Tina and Sara, you remember how to put the bait on the hook.

Sara: I need help, Grandpa.

Tina: I do too. Please help me after you get the bait on Sara's hook.

GP: I will help you both right now.

(Susan and Taavi help the girls cast the lines and reel them in. After an hour and a half, the girls are tired.)

Susan: Did you girls enjoy catching those tiny fish?

Tina and Sara: Yes, Grandma. We wish that the fish had been bigger so Grandpa could have fried them.

GP: Yes, girls. But, you caught something. Those fish that you let go back into the water will grow up. In a year or two, you may catch them again. Then, they will be big enough to eat.

Susan: Sara and Tina, let's help Grandpa take the fishing rods back to the shed.

Scene V: Family gets ready for the pool. Everyone swims for a few hours.

GP: Is anyone hungry yet?

Susan: We all are. When can we have lunch?

Taavi: I'm going to prepare some frozen fish from the store. Also, there will be fresh vegetables and corn on the cob.

Scene VI: Family eats together. The girls help Susan clean up. The family goes for a nap.

Scene VII: After napping, there are board games for everyone. After a few hours, Susan and Taavi begin to prepare the **Sabbath Feast**. Rachel then arrives and helps to prepare the meal also.

Scene VIII: The **Sabbath (feast) supper**. There is scripture reading, prayers, lighting of candles, blessing on the family and blessing of the food.

GP: Girls, please find a seat. We are going to begin our **Shabbat meal.** Taavi puts on **kipa**.

Taavi: Let's read the first scripture: **Lev. 23:3**: "Work six days. The seventh day is a **Sabbath,** a day of total and complete rest, a **sacred assembly**. Don't do any work. Wherever you live, it is a **Sabbath to God**." ("**The Message**)"

(The Father Begins by Reading): **John 8:12**, then **Mark 12:29-31**: Jesus said, "The first in importance is, 'Listen, Israel: **The Lord your God** is one: so love the **Lord God** with all your passion and prayer and intelligence and energy.' And here is the second: 'Love others as well as you love yourself.' There is no other commandment that ranks with these." (**"The Message"**)

There is a prayer: "Abba, we now put aside all cares, and turn our hearts to You, as we enter **Your Shabbat**, the rest you have ordained for our good. Truly, this is the day that you have made, and we will rejoice and be glad in it."

(Lighting of the Candles). The candlesticks represent: One for Ephraim and one for Judah. One for Heaven and one for Earth. One for the King and one for His servants. One candle stands for the Tanach (Old Covenant), and one for the Brit Hadasha (New Covenant). One is for faith and one for holy deeds. One for work and one for rest. Both symbolize commandments in **Mark 12:29-31**.

Then, Taavi says: Susan, please light the candles and say the prayer, with the girls:

"Barukh atah Adonai Eloheinu Melekh Ha-olam, asher kideshanu bemitz votav ve-tzivanu lehiyot or la-goyim v'natan-lanu et **Yeshua Meshicheinu or ha-olam. Amein."**

"Blessed are You, Lord our God, King of the Universe, Who sanctified us with **Your Commandments**, and commanded us to be a **light to the nations** and Who gave to us **Yeshua our Messiah, the Light of the world. Amen."**

Then, the Mother's Prayer:

Susan: (praying): "**God of Abraham, Isaac, and Jacob**. You are holy and You have consecrated the **Shabbat**, and give it to Your people, Israel, as a sign throughout the generations as an everlasting covenant. You have commanded us to honor **Your Sabbath**, with light, with joy, and with peace. As we light these candles, may one represent **Yeshua** as the **light of the world** and the other **His light** that is in us, His servants. **Almighty Father**, I ask that you grant me and my loved ones a chance to truly enter into **Your rest** on the **Sabbath** day. Even as the candles give light to our family, so may Your **Ruach HaKodesh** (Holy Spirit) gives light to our home and lives. **Father,** I ask that **You** make your **Presence** known in our home, and that you bless our children and grandchildren with wisdom, knowledge and understanding of **You**. By the empowerment of **Your grace** may they always walk in the ways of **Torah, Your light**. May you ever be their **GOD** and mine, **O LORD, My Creator, and Redeemer. The Mighty One of Israel. Amen."**

Washing of Hands

Grandpa pours water from a pitcher to wash his hands (and family follows) as he says the blessing:" "**Baruch Atah Adonai Elohenu Melech Ha-olam**, Asher kidshanu bemeetz votav, vetzee vanu al neteelat Yadayim." "Blessed are You o **Lord our God, King of the Universe**, who sanctifies us with your commandments, and has commanded us regarding washing of hands.

Hamotzi Blessing of the Bread

"A reading from **John 6:35**." Then, prayer in Hebrew": "**Baruch atah Adonai, Eloheinu Melech Ha-olam**, hamotzi lechem min ha aretz, lechem chaim **b'Yeshua. Amein."**

"**Blessed are You, LORD our GOD, King of the Universe,** who blesses us with bread, the **Bread of Life in Yeshua. Amen."**

"Then, **John 7:37-38** is read."

Kiddush Sanctifying Prayer

(Father reads):

"**Baruch** atah **Adonai, Elohenu** melech ha olam, borei p'ri ha agaphen. **Amein**."

"**Blessed are You, O LORD our GOD, King of the Universe**, who gives us the fruit of the vine."

Blessing Over the Children

Over the son, The Father Prays:

"**Y'simech Elohim K'Ephrayeem, v'chee M'nasheh."**

"May God make you a symbol of blessing as He did Ephraim and Manasseh."

Over the daughter and granddaughters, The Mother (Grandmother) prays:

"Y'simech **Elohim** K'Sarah, Rivka, Rakhel v'Leah."

"May **GOD** make you a symbol of blessing as He did Sarah, Rebekah, Rachel and Leah."

Sara recites Ephesians 6: 1-3.

Husband Blesses His Wife.

He reads **Proverbs 31:10-31** (or another Scripture).

Wife Blesses Her Husband.

She reads **Psalm 1 or 119** (or another Scripture).

ALL SING THE SHEMA

"**Sh'ma Yisrael, Adonai Elohenu, Adonai Echod. Baruch shem, K'vod malchuto**, l'olam voed."

"Hear O Israel**, the Lord our God. The Lord is One. Blessed be His Name. His Kingdom is forever**, and forever more." **(Mark 12:29)**

FATHER GIVES PRIESTLY BLESSING:

"Yevarech'cha **Adonai** v'yishmerech Ya'er **Adonai** panav eleycha biyechuneka **Yissah Adonai** panav eleycha veyasem lecha shalom."

"May **the Lord** bless you and keep you. May **the Lord** cause His face to shine upon you and be gracious unto you. May **the Lord** lift up His countenance upon you and give you peace." (Num. 6:24-26)

Shabbat Shalom (Sabbath Peace)

(The family has chicken with potato salad, baked beans, and challah bread. Also, the adults have red wine. The children have grape juice.)

Scene IX: After the girls brush their teeth, Grandmother puts the girls to bed. Grandfather comes in to pray with the girls. Everyone retires for the night.

GP: Let us pray: "**Heavenly Father**, our **Adonai,** we thank You for this Sabbath. We bless **Your Holy Name** and thank you for this day of rest. Give us peaceful sleep, we pray. In the name of **Yeshua, our Messiah. Amein**."

ACT V

Morning devotions, boating, swimming, and Sabbath service.

Scene I: Family again gets juice, milk, coffee, tea or water. They assemble in the family room. This is Saturday.

Taavi: Good morning family. Shalom (peace). I pray that you all had a good night sleep.

Tina: It was a very sound sleep, Grandpa.

Sara: I really enjoyed the rest last night. It was very peaceful.

Susan: I had a pleasant time of resting.

GP: I slept through the night, but had to get up to give the creature kids, Gordie and Missy, a treat several times.

GP: Let's begin by singing some more Messianic Christian songs. (Taavi picks out four songs in Hebrew and English.) The singing is completed.

Susan: The girls pronounced the Hebrew very well. I'm proud of both of you.

Taavi: Let's finish the book of James, which we started discussing several days ago. Susan, please read after me, verses 16 – 18. Tina can you and Sara read verses 19 and 20, please, after Grandma finishes her verses. Let's begin to read **James 5:13-20:**

"Are you hurting? Pray. Do you feel great? Sing. Are you sick? Call the church leaders together to pray and anoint you with oil in the name of the **Master**. Believing prayer will heal you, and **Jesus** will put you on your feet. And if you've sinned, you'll be forgiven—healed inside and out." **(verses 13 -15) ("The Message")**

Susan: (continuing to read): "Make this your common practice. Confess your sins to each other and pray for each other so that you can live together whole and healed. The prayer of a person living right with God is something powerful to be reckoned with. Elijah, for instance, human like us, prayed hard that it wouldn't rain, and it didn't—not a drop for three and a half years. Then he prayed that it would rain, and it did. The showers came and everything started growing again." **(verses 16-18) ("The Message")**

Tina: (continuing to read): "My dear friends, if you know people who have wandered off from **God's truth**, don't write them off. Go after them." **(verse 19) ("The Message")**

Sara: (finishing the chapter): "Get them back and you will have rescued precious lives from destruction and prevented an epidemic of wandering away from **God.**" (**verse 20**) ("**The Message**")

GP: Anyone have any comments about any of the verses.

Susan: Yes, Taavi. I like the part in verse 13, where you can call the church elders together and have prayer by anointing with oil to be healed, according to the will of **Yeshua.**

Tina: I like the idea of being well and healed.

Sara: I have friends who have wandered away from the Lord. Their lives are miserable.

GP: Let's pray for our family and friends that they will draw closer to the **Lord** and experience wellness and peace in their lives again. Susan, would you begin?

Susan: We thank you **Heavenly Father** for this visit with Tina and Sara. We pray that they will enjoy this **Sabbath** day. We ask that our children and daughter-in-law and Tina and Sara and our other grandchildren will live prosperous, healthy, and peaceful lives. Bless each of them we pray, in the name of **Adonai.** Give Tina and Sara wisdom on praying and witnessing to their friends, we pray. **Amen.**

Scene II: Grandpa fixes breakfast of French toast, eggs, cereal and fruit. Everyone talks about the last few days and how much they have enjoyed the unique experiences.

GP: Let's clean up the dishes. I will meet you all on the boat.

Today will be a cruise up and down the lake with no camera or fishing poles. I want us to enjoy the ride without any distractions. We will have our cell phones if we see anything exciting to photograph.

And, Susan, please make sure everyone has applied sunscreen. I'll get the cooler and the drinks. Tina, please bring Missy.

Scene III: Family assembles on the pontoon boat with Missy. The captain, Taavi, checks the life jackets and makes sure Missy, the dog, is secured.

Taavi: Ok, let's enjoy the boat ride. A prayer: "Thank you **Lord** that there is a little breeze today. Give us **safety** and **Your protection**. Give me alertness, I pray. In the name of **Yeshua, Amein.**"

Tina: This lake is so beautiful. There are a lot of cypress trees and water fowl up and down the lake.

Sara: I really enjoy the pretty houses and docks and boats that are on the lake.

GP: **Praise the Lord**. We are also owners of the lake and have lakefront property and a dock to park our boat.

Susan: Can we go slowly back to the other end of the lake.

Taavi: Yes, Susan. I will gear down to between 2500 and 3000 RPM. When we come back, is it alright if I put the boat back in the dock?

Susan: Yes, it is alright with me.

GP: Would you girls like us to attach the raft to the boat?

Sara: I would like to do that.

Tina: I'll watch Sara first.

(Taavi and Susan hook the ropes to the boat and the raft.)

GP: I'll go the same speed to which I just geared down.

Susan: Are you having fun Sara?

Sara: Yes. Is it alright if Tina joins me now?

Susan: Let me ask. Tina, your sister would like you to join her on the raft. Do you feel secure now?

Tina: Yes, Grandma.

(Taavi stops the boat and reels in the raft. Tina is placed beside Sara securely. Both have on their life jackets. The ropes are checked to be clear of the motor.)

GP: After we go up one time more, we'll head back to the dock.

(After going up the lake and back, Taavi stops the boat near the dock and, along with Susan, helps the girls get back in the boat. The raft is secured. Taavi parks the boat.)

Scene IV: The girls and Susan go to the pool, while Taavi barbeques the lunch.

Taavi: Lunch is served. We can eat on the patio tables today if everyone is okay with the idea.

Susan: That is a splendid idea. I will also get paper plates, plastic silverware, plastic cups and napkins.

Tina: I would like to pray for lunch. "**Lord Jesus**, thank You for such a beautiful day. We had a lot of fun. Bless Grandpa and Grandma for all they have done for us. **In Jesus name, Amen**."

Taavi: Thank you, Tina. You and Sara can pray anytime you want. We appreciate and love both of you very much.

Scene V: After cleaning up the patio tables after lunch, the family takes a nap to get ready for **Shabbat service** at 5 P.M.

GP: Let's all take a rest. It's 3 P.M. now. I will awaken you at 3:45 P.M. We will leave for the sanctuary at 4:20 P.M.

Scene VI: After napping, the family gets up and prepares to go to **Shabbat service**.

Susan: Are you almost ready girls? Are you ready Taavi?

Tina and Sara: Yes Grandma.

Taavi: I'm ready to get into the car. Everyone, let's go!

Scene VII: The family arrives at **Beit Tikkun** at 5 P.M. Grandpa Taavi puts on his **tallit** and **kipa**.

There is a praise and worship service before the teaching. Then, Rabbi Ya'akov and his wife, Pastor Debra, begin the service.

Pastor Debra prays. Then, an offering is collected. There is a break of five minutes to greet friends. Then Rabbi calls us to order for the **Parsha** (Torah Portion) for the **Shabbat service**.

Rabbi Ya'akov: "Welcome. This week's **Parsha** is called Eikev (Because)." The scripture portion is:

" And this is what will happen, because [**eikev**[: When you , on your part, will obey these directives, keeping and following them, **God** on his part, will keep the covenant [**brit**] of loyal love [**chesed**-mercy] that he made with your ancestors: **He** will love you, he will bless you, and he will increase you." (Deut. 7:12 -13) (**"The Message"**)

"Last week, Parsha Va'etchanan, Moses reviewed the **Torah** and repeated the **Ten Commandments…"**

" This week, in Parsha Eikev, Moses continues with this theme, promising the Israelites that they would enjoy prosperity and good health if they walk in **God's ways**."

Moses indicates that we cannot only be hearers of the **Word of God**, but also, "diligent doers."

"The blessings and benefits" that we receive from **our God** are due to our "obedience to **His Word**."

This Parsha states that there are "rewards" that are "brought about by obedience": they are "prosperity, favor and good health":

" **God** will get rid of all sickness." (Deut 7:15) (**"The Message"**)

"When **God** makes a covenant, He doesn't break it."

"And he remembers, remembers **his Covenant**…the **Covenant** he made with Abraham, the same oath he swore to Isaac, The very statute he established with Jacob, the **Eternal Covenant** with Israel. Namely, 'I give you the land. Canaan is your hill-country inheritance.'" Psalm 105:8-11 (**"The Message"**)

It is important to know that by honoring " our covenant with **God** " that we choose to love **Him** and to keep **His commandments**, "not only do we receive **God's blessing** on our own lives," our children do also, and our children's children, "to a thousand generations down the line!"

"Know this: **God**, **your God**, **is God indeed**, **a God** you can depend upon. He keeps the covenant of loyal love with those who love him and observe his commandments for a thousand generations." (Deut. 7:9) (**"The Message"**)

Later on in the sermon, Rabbi shares this information: "The Hebrew word for desert or wilderness is **midbar**, which has the same root letters as **m'daber** (to speak)."

God's word sustains us, and He often speaks to us during our "desert times of spiritual dryness."

There in our desert, we receive testing "so that he would know what you were made of, whether you would keep his commandments or not." (Deut. 8:2) (**"The Message"**)

"The rabbis call this testing 'chastisements of love.'"

"It's the child he loves that he disciplines; the child he embraces, he also corrects." (Hebrews 12:6) (**"The Message"**)

…"His discipline is not only strict and just, but also merciful and tender."

"Consider it a sheer gift, friends, when tests and challenges come at you from all sides. You know that under pressure, your faith-life is forced into the open and shows its true colors." (James 1:2) ("The **Message"**)

…"When we are confronted by a sense of our own unworthiness, ashamed by our sinfulness—our stubbornness and rebellion—we can still count on **God's faithfulness** to the covenant we have with **Him** through **Yeshua HaMashiach** (Jesus the Messiah)."

In further closing remarks, Rabbi stated: "Because of our covenant relationship with **Him, God** will never leave us nor forsake us."

"Bring your full tithe to the **Temple treasury** so there will be ample provisions in my **Temple**. Test me in this and see if I don't open up heaven itself to you and pour out blessings beyond your wildest dreams." (Malachai 3:9-10) (**"The Message"**)

Rabbi Ya'akov leads in prayer and dismisses us.

(Rabbi Ya'akov and Pastor Debra comment on how well-mannered and attentive that Sara and Tina were during the sermon.)

Scene VIII: The family again goes to "Steak 'N Shake." They enjoy their meal together; and, then, drive home.

Taavi: Tina and Sara, was the Shabbat an interesting experience?

Tina: Yes, I enjoyed the flag ceremony during the song service.

Sara: I found it very interesting how the young ladies had such a great skill.

Susan: (after arriving back home): Let's go to bed after you brush your teeth and say your prayers. Tomorrow, we can get up later. Be blessed tonight as you rest.

Taavi: Goodnight girls. Sleep in Heavenly Peace!

THE END

EPILOGUE

The family is a very important unit today and in our world's civilization history.

Today, with many families lacking a father or mother, grandfather or grandmother, the good times described in the book, between grandparents and grandchildren, are enlightening and encouraging.

Would that families could be whole, and based on Christian principles, thrive.

Basic human contentment involves peace, joy and love.

Taavi and Susan and Tina and Sara share some wonderful days of vacation together on the lake.

I chose **the book of James** to show that, even though there are problems and misbehavior in the **body of Christ**, these issues can be exposed and resolved.

Good pastors and rabbis will stand against unbelief and disorder. They will be able to analyze, confront and solve issues effectively.

Righteous living can be maintained by constant devotion and assembling ourselves together in a worship setting.

The power of the **Holy Spirit** is evident in the Messianic Christian congregation of Beit Tikkun, where the Mohlers attend services. Rabbi Ya'akov and his wife, Pastor Debra are loving and caring people who shepherd their flock carefully and with great compassion.

I hope you have enjoyed this story of grandparents and grandchildren, who love **the Lord** and each other.

May you be richly blessed!

The author

Printed in the United States
by Baker & Taylor Publisher Services